PU

HENRY AND THE SEA

Henry moves to the seaside with his parents, but takes no notice of the Sea, preferring to play video games. One day, the Sea talks to Henry and decides to take a holiday, accompanying him to hospital in London. The Sea is bored and miserable at the way humans treat it and Henry is going to London for important tests as he is very ill, so they could both do with some company. An exciting friendship develops which takes Henry and the Sea to some rather unusual places and leaves the world wondering where the waves went.

Alexander Stuart's five-year-old son, Joe Buffalo, first had the idea of talking to the Sea and together they wrote this book. At the time, Joe Buffalo was ill with a rare form of cancer and, though he saw the pictures, sadly he died before his book could be published. Joe said that he wanted to become a seagull when he died, so perhaps he still flies over Brighton where his mother and father live? Alexander Stuart is the author of one other children's book, *Joe, Jo-Jo and the Monkey Masks*.

HENRY AND THE SEA

JOE BUFFALO STUART
and ALEXANDER STUART

Illustrated by Teri Gower

PUFFIN BOOKS

PUFFIN BOOKS

Published by the Penguin Group
Penguin Books Ltd, 27 Wrights Lane, London w8 5tz, England
Viking Penguin, a division of Penguin Books USA Inc.
375 Hudson Street, New York, New York 10014, USA
Penguin Books Australia Ltd, Ringwood, Victoria, Australia
Penguin Books Canada Ltd, 2801 John Street, Markham, Ontario, Canada l3r 1b4
Penguin Books (NZ) Ltd, 182–190 Wairau Road, Auckland 10, New Zealand

Penguin Books Ltd, Registered Offices: Harmondsworth, Middlesex, England

First published by Hamish Hamilton Children's Books 1989
Published in Puffin Books 1991
1 3 5 7 9 10 8 6 4 2

Text copyright © Joe Buffalo Stuart and Alexander Stuart, 1989
Illustrations copyright © Teri Gower, 1989
All rights reserved

Printed in England by Clays Ltd, St Ives plc
Filmset in Baskerville

For Mummy,
from Joe

This book is dedicated with love to the children and staff of
Kenneth Grahame Ward, St Stephen's Hospital, London;
Plymouth Ward, Charing Cross Hospital, London; the
Physiotherapy Department and Cawthorne Ward, the Royal
Alexandra Hospital for Sick Children, Brighton; and with
much gratitude to the National Health Service, long may it
survive.

A.S.

A Very Healthy Place

WHEN HENRY WENT to live by the sea, everyone said it was for his health. Which it was. Henry had never seen a healthier place: video games on the pier; hot dogs and fish and chips and hamburgers and sticks of rock and candy floss; healthy outdoor sports like riding the ghost train past bone people and blood people and worse. There was even a site of historical healthy importance – an old Victorian sewage pipe which at low tide filled the air with a rich and possibly historical stench.

I

Henry went down to the seafront
every day after school, but he hardly
ever noticed the sea. Inside the
Pleasuredome on the pier, which
Henry called the Circus, he couldn't
even hear the sea for all the electronic
beepings and clangings and
racketings, and he couldn't see it for
the haze of cigarette smoke. Even
outside, if he concentrated very hard
on the shooting gallery and the coin-
operated motorbikes and the helter-
skelter and the dodgem cars, it wasn't
too difficult for Henry to forget

altogether that the sea was there.

Until one day he heard a voice – a low, rumbling, almost sloshing voice which said, "Ah-hm, I am here, you know."

But Henry didn't. He didn't know and he didn't particularly care. He was too busy pushing a coin into a remote-controlled motorboat which he hoped to send smashing into all the others.

"Me. I'm right underneath you. I am here, you know," the voice went on.

And Henry looked down. There, through the cracks in the old wooden boards of the pier, Henry could see where he thought the voice was coming from – a sort of glinting, sparkling, lapping wetness that he seemed to remember washed right up on to the beach and then rolled back again.

"That's right," the Sea said. "It's me. You're quite privileged to hear this, you know."

But Henry said, "I'm busy now." And he slid the coin into the slot and started working the control of the motorboat, steering it straight across the bow of a police boat.

"Oh, carry on then," said the Sea in a gloomy, rather sorry-for-itself kind of way and it broke against the pier legs a couple of times, slapping

hard on the old metal so that Henry
felt the force of its waves. "Don't
mind me," it said. "I was here before
any of this whojamaflip. I know it's
all very entertaining, but it wouldn't
be quite the same without me, would
it?"

"Not now!" Henry shouted. "Not
now! I'm just going to go straight for
that big car ferry and – " But his

5

money ran out and the motorboat slowed and stopped.

"Sea!" he said threateningly through the cracks in the pier, grinding his shoe on the wood to make his point. "Sea! Look what you made me do. You made me miss it. My money ran out. I didn't hit the ferry."

"Very sorry, I'm sure," sloshed the Sea.

"What are you bothering me for?" Henry asked. "Why don't you go and bother someone else? Look – there are hundreds of other children around, or there's that old woman over there. Go and tell her your troubles. You're making me very, very angry!"

Henry meant this. He stomped his feet on the boards and marched up and down a few times with an angry

black cloud hanging over his head to
prove it. He marched all the way
round the outside of the Circus,
fuming so hard that he got the sun to
disappear for a moment. He marched
straight to the end of the pier and
stuck his nose out in front of him and
stared at – he stared at – at – the Sea.

Do Seagulls Think?

"ARE YOU QUITE finished?" asked the Sea. "Have you always had a temper like that or is it something you've practised? You're quite an objectionable little character when you want to be, aren't you?"

"Yes," said Henry proudly, staring out at the waves and screwing his eyes up in an evil grin. "Yes, I am."

"You come here a lot. I've seen you every day."

"I live here now," Henry said. He put his hand in his pocket and felt the coins there. Three more video games

or two and an ice-cream. He turned to
go.

"Aren't you a little young to come
on your own?" the Sea asked.

"My mum and dad are right here
with me," Henry said. "Didn't you
notice? Dad doesn't say a lot. He's too
busy writing this down – and carrying
my bicycle. And Mum doesn't like the
pier much."

"I don't blame her," the Sea said
as Henry ventured back inside the fog
of the Circus. "Why don't you come
down on the beach so we can have a

proper conversation? It's not easy making myself heard above all these machines and that music and everything. Even the seagulls can't hear themselves think."

"Do they?" Henry asked, playing his favourite video game and getting roasted by a dragon.

"DO THEY WHAT?" the Sea shouted above the din.

"Think," Henry said.

"WHAT?" the Sea shouted.

"Do seagulls think?" Henry asked, trying the game again and getting burnt a second time.

"Not much," the Sea admitted as Henry came back outside and bought an ice-lolly with the last of his change. "About fish mostly. They're not very good at conversation. Have you ever tried talking to a seagull? Boring. But at least they try, at least they don't spend their time staring at a stupid little video screen. Now, come down on the beach and stand right there!"

"Where?" Henry asked, realising he had no money left for anything on the pier.

"There," the Sea said, as Henry walked down the stone steps and across the pebbles to where it had made them dark and wet. "Keep your feet still and then see how fast you can move when I roll back in."

"Why would I want to do that?" Henry asked.

"It's a game," the Sea explained, rather doubtfully. "I might catch you out. And then you'll have wet feet."

"Very funny," Henry muttered in a mocking tone. "Is that the best you can do? What a great sense of humour you've got!" And he flicked his lolly stick as far as he could out across the water.

"I'M NOT A RUBBISH BIN!" the Sea roared, crashing over the pebbles and foaming at the mouth. Then just to show that it really did have a sense of humour, it built itself up into a truly monstrous wave and let it break close to Henry, sending a whole jumble of seaweed and flapping fish and Henry's lolly stick and even a swimmer or two flying through the air, right over his head, and totally drenching Henry and Henry's mum and dad in the process.

"Very funny," Henry said, helping his mother untangle an eel from her hair and unpinching a crab from his dad's nose. "My dad's funnier than you when he's asleep!"

The Sea Goes Whoosh

"YOU'RE NOT GOING, are you?" the Sea asked worriedly when Henry started walking back up the beach. "Do I bore you?"

"I've got things to do!" Henry said, stopping and picking up a flat pebble that looked like a squashed hamburger bun. "We're going to London tomorrow to hospital for some tests to make sure that I'm all right."

"Why wouldn't you be?" the Sea wanted to know.

"I had a bug inside me," Henry said. "Not a real bug – not like a stag

16

beetle or anything. It's gone now, they think."

"What is a stag beetle?" the Sea asked, sounding puzzled.

Henry thought. "Sort of a strange black crab or a lobster – or worse!" he said.

"Worse?" the Sea said, knowing what it feels like to have strange creatures with claws crawling about inside you.

"But that's what it wasn't," Henry pointed out.

"All the same," the Sea said, "I think I should come with you."

"What?" said Henry.

"I want to come with you."

Henry tossed the flat pebble in his hand a couple of times, then spun it out across the waves, trying to make it bounce from one to another. It wasn't quite as good as getting roasted by a huge video dragon, but it passed the time. "Where?" he asked.

"To the hospital," said the Sea. "To London. I've never been there."

"Of course you've never been there!" Henry said. "You're the Sea! You've never been to lots of places that aren't on the coast!"

Actually the Sea had, but that was a very long time ago and it didn't want to confuse things so it said, "Well, I'd like to come," sounding dark and gloomy and sorrowful, the way it did when it wanted to get its own way. "Ouch!"

"I thought the pebbles couldn't hurt you," said Henry, who had just thrown a big one. "I thought they were all part of your natural wonder."

"Well, you were wrong," the Sea

18

said, letting its voice sink down and down.

"Anyway, you can't," Henry said.

"Why not?" asked the Sea.

"You're too big. How could I take you with me?"

"I could flow up the drains and water pipes to London," the Sea suggested, brightening a little and turning green and sparkly in the sunlight. "I could wash right into the hospital. It does have radiator pipes and sinks and things like that?"

"Yes," said Henry.

"I could be right in your room with you when you have the tests."

"I'd like that," admitted Henry.

"Or there is a simpler way," the Sea told him, stretching itself out over the pebbles in a fine, white, bubbly line.

"What's that?"

"A little party trick," said the Sea. "Something I've been meaning to try for a long time. I need a holiday – all this rolling in, rolling out, it gets to you after a few hundred million years. You see that old plastic coffee cup there, washed up on the beach?"

"The one with the lid?" said Henry.

"That's the one. Pick it up, will you?"

"Yes," said Henry. And he did, snapping off the plastic lid and tipping out the crab which was hiding inside.

"Right. Hold it just about there," the Sea told him. And while Henry watched, there was a huge whooshing sound – like a thousand waves all breaking at once, or a million toilets all flushing – and suddenly the Sea

21

disappeared inside the slightly crumpled white cup in Henry's hand.

All of it.

Suddenly there was no Sea. Just a beach stretching as far as Henry's eyes could see. Suddenly there were no swimmers or windsurfers or yachts. Just idiotic-looking people flailing about in puddles on the sand – for where the Sea had been, there was sand, not pebbles. Henry looked and looked again. Still he could not believe it.

Until a voice from inside the cup said, "Close your mouth, will you? You look like a fish and I'd rather like a break from those. And take that foolish expression off your face. People will start to talk."

"Is that you?" Henry asked, staring down at the tiny waves lapping at the side of the cup. "What happened to the rest of you – the big bit?"

"Ah," said the Sea. "When you've been around as long as I have, you learn a thing or two. Now snap the lid on and take me home fast. We've got a journey ahead of us tomorrow."

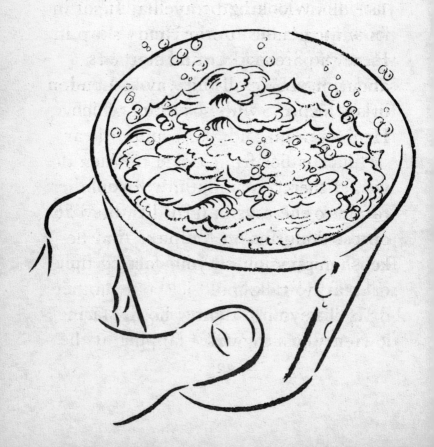

Why Are All Those Seagulls
Following Us?

THE SEA WAS a bad traveller. It sat in its white plastic cup in Henry's lap in Henry's parents' car and sloshed about, moaning all the way to London in a whispery, whooshy voice which Henry's mum and dad couldn't hear.

"This is boring," it said. "When do we get there? Why doesn't your father ram into the cars in front like they do on the dodgems on the pier? And he keeps missing everything coming the other way! He should let your mother drive if he doesn't know how."

Henry just giggled.

But then he heard something on the car radio which made him sit up and listen. A voice which seemed to be struggling to speak through a mouthful of prunes announced:

'In a dramatic turn of events late last night, it was revealed that an international task force of scientists has been called in to tackle the knotty problem of what has happened to the sea. Experts are baffled by the mystery disappearance and admit they have no idea where the sea went – or why. As a result of the Big Wet One's shock vanishing act, world shipping has literally ground to a halt and we have received confirmation from the Russian cosmonaut currently orbiting the earth in Glasnost-4 that our planet has lost all its blue bits! Some observers believe

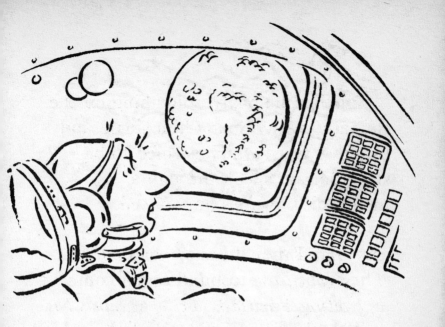

that this is all the result of the so-called Greenhouse Effect, caused by the increase in the sun's heat due to the reduced ozone layer in the atmosphere, but other scientists admit that on this one, they've been left high and dry!'

"I don't know what everyone is complaining about," grumbled Henry's dad at the wheel. "Now we can drive to China if we want to – or Africa or America. Think of all the

27

extra land they'll have available.
They'll be able to build a golf course
in every garden!"

"It's the fish I worry about," said
Henry's mum. "And the whales and
dolphins. They say the sea's left deep
puddles where they can survive – but
for how long?"

"I'm just taking a holiday," the Sea
said, slapping against the side of
Henry's white plastic cup. "Does
anyone object? I mean, I haven't had
a day off in years!"

"It's funny," said Henry's mum,
who couldn't really hear what the Sea

was saying. "You don't really notice
something until it's gone. I keep
thinking I can hear the waves
breaking, even here on the
motorway."

"What I don't understand," said
Henry's dad, peering up through the
windscreen, "is why all those seagulls
are following us. There must be
hundreds of them, making a mess on
the car. I only washed it yesterday!"

And Henry said nothing.

A Treasure-Map Island

AT THE HOSPITAL, Henry placed the
Sea carefully on a cabinet next to the
big scanning machine they were going
to use on him. A nurse scowled at the
crumpled plastic cup with distaste.

"You can't have that in here," she
said. "It's not clean. No knowing
where that's been. Dirty water breeds
germs!" And she went to pick it up.

"Don't!" Henry said. But he
couldn't think of anything else to say
after that, so he just screamed and
screamed so fiercely that thè nurse

30

had to put down the cup to cover her ears.

"Well, I don't know what the doctor will say," she told him crossly and marched out of the room, shaking her head.

"That was a close call," whispered the Sea. But Henry, who had had an injection, was drifting off to sleep.

Henry had to lie still under the scanning machine for a very long time and he half-knew where he was and half-didn't. Every now and then, the lights on the equipment overhead would blink, or he would feel the mattress he was lying on being moved by the machine, so that some of the time he thought he was an astronaut in a space capsule and some of the time he thought he was a sailor on the sea.

And even though he was half-
asleep, he found that he could talk to
the Sea better than ever.

"I went to a treasure-map island for

a holiday once," Henry said, "and the sea there was really hot. Was that you?" he asked. "I mean was it the same sea, Sea?"

"Oh, yes," rumbled the Sea. "I'm warmer in places than in others, and people do talk about there being seven of me, but basically it's all me. Even I lose track of all the places I am sometimes," it went on. "If you divided the world's surface into three parts, I'd cover more than two of them, you know!"

And Henry said, "But you don't actually do much, do you, Sea? I mean, all this rolling in and out. It doesn't really get you anywhere, does it?"

"It's not my fault," replied the Sea, a little huffily. "The moon never stops pulling and pushing me about. What with that and the winds, I've often thought about disappearing like this for good!"

"But you are going back?" Henry said.

"No, I'm not," sloshed the Sea. "I'm staying with you for quite a long time."

"Well, you can't," said Henry drowsily. "You know that – it's just not possible." He drifted for a moment on the waves under the scanner. "Anyway," he went on, "what I don't understand is this: if you're so big and powerful and important, what are you doing here talking to me?"

But Henry was washing further and further into sleep, so that he didn't hear the Sea tell him, "Because you're my friend . . ."

Something Terrible Happens

WHEN HENRY WOKE up, he was in another room and he noticed immediately that the white plastic cup was gone.

"Oh no," he said to his mother, who was sitting with him. "What did they do with it?"

"What, dear?" asked Henry's mum.

"The Sea!" said Henry. "The Sea! Where's it gone?"

"That's what everybody wants to know," said Henry's dad, coming through the door. "It's all over the newspapers and TV," he said,

switching the hospital's television on.
A woman with two wobbly faces
and green hair was reading the news:

'*In a dramatic turn of events late last
night, it was revealed that detectives
with tracker dogs have been brought in
to hunt for the missing sea. Witnesses
to the disappearance claim they last
saw the sea destroying children's sand
castles on several beaches and police*

warn that, if spotted, the sea may be
dangerous and should not be
approached. An official police
spokesperson admitted, however, that,
"Frankly, on this one, we're out of our
depth!" '

"Where is it?" Henry was shrieking.
"We had it with us – in the white
plastic cup!"

"Oh that," said Henry's mum.

"What's he on about?" asked
Henry's dad.

"I don't know what you were
thinking of, bringing that filthy old
cup here with you," Henry's mum
was saying. "I asked a nurse to throw
it away."

"You WHAT?" burbled Henry,
sitting up in bed. "You – asked –
a – ??" He slumped back on to the

37

pillow. "This is terrible," he said weakly. "We've got to do something."

"Is it just me?" his father was saying to his mother. "Or is he really not making any sense? Do you think we should call a doctor?"

But Henry, who was lying back trying to imagine where on earth his poor friend could be right now – in the drains? in the sewer? – suddenly heard a tapping sound coming from the big, white hospital sink by his bed. It wasn't so much a tapping as a rattling, followed by a loud WHOOSH! and a gurgle, like a pipe burping.

"There must be something blocking that sink," said Henry's father, and he came over to take a look.

Henry pushed himself up on to one elbow. "Could it be . . . ?" he wondered.

"Hospital plumbing!" remarked Henry's dad disgustedly, peering down the plug hole and twisting his nose at the faint briny smell coming from it. "Just needs a good jet of water to clear it – "

But before his hand could reach the tap, Henry had swung his legs out of bed and was trying to stand, shouting, "WHATEVER YOU DO, DON'T TURN ON THE WATER!"

Henry's father blinked in

astonishment. It had been a strange day – and now his son was behaving most peculiarly.

"It's all right," Henry said, doing his best to reassure him. "I want to do it. I just want a drink." And he put himself between the tap and his dad.

"I could have got you a drink," Henry's father said, shaking his head as if nothing made much sense any more. "I would have got him a drink," he repeated to Henry's mum, but then they both lost themselves watching the weather forecast on TV.

Henry gazed at the sink.

"Ah-hm," came the voice. "Had you worried, didn't I? Definitely got you going for a moment there, didn't I?" And it chuckled, in a wet, sloshy sort of way.

"Sea!" Henry said, pulling himself up to lean over the edge of the sink. "Sea!" he growled, trying to look menacing even though he was grinning all over his face. "Don't ever do that again!"

"Do what?" asked the Sea, all innocence. "It's not my fault. I wasn't the one snoring away under the

41

scanner. I didn't ask to be tipped out of my nice comfortable cup – I was lucky this sink had a big U-bend I could settle in, otherwise who knows where I'd be now!"

"Sea," Henry said, glancing round to see if his parents were watching him, but they were still engrossed in the weather maps on TV. "Sea, I don't know what I'm going to do with you . . . " And he didn't; he was already wondering what he could find in the hospital room to carry his friend back home in. "But I'm glad you're here."

The Seagulls Are Back

THE SEA DID nothing but complain about Henry's solution to the problem of how to get it home.

"I thought you had such a terrific sense of humour," Henry teased. "I don't hear you laughing."

"It simply isn't funny, that's why," said the Sea in a huffy sort of way. "Surely you could have found something more . . ."

"Yes?" said Henry, enjoying himself.

" . . . more suitable?" said the Sea.

"I don't see what's unsuitable

about a urine bottle," Henry said. "I have to use them all the time in hospital. You're lucky I managed to smuggle this one into the car. I don't think Dad would be too keen to hear you sloshing about in there."

But there wasn't much chance of that. Henry's father, once again, was cursing the cloud of seagulls which threatened to engulf the car as it sped home along the motorway.

"Look at them!" he was muttering. "How many more can there be up there? I think we must have every scrawny bird in the country following us. I feel like the Pied Piper. I'm surprised the police don't stop us – I can't see where we're going, I just turn the wheel every time someone blasts his horn!"

And as if they had heard what his dad said, Henry noticed now that

there was the sound of a siren somewhere behind them, mingling with the screeching of the seagulls, fading in and fading out as the car rocked from side to side and the Sea lapped grumpily at the papier-mâché urine bottle.

> *'In a dramatic turn of events late last night – '*

Henry's mum had just turned on the car radio –

> *'the Prime Minister told Parliament that the disappearance of the sea was the best thing that could have happened to the country. "For too long," she said, "the ocean has taken advantage of British beaches and the goodwill of the British people. As far as I'm*

*concerned, it's good riddance to bad
rubbish. Now we'll be able to build
more housing, more roads, more
schools, more office blocks, more
supermarkets . . . " '*

"And more golf courses," echoed
Henry's dad, desperately trying to get
the windscreen wipers to clear the
shower of seagull droppings.
 "She can't mean that!" Henry
protested. "No one can be glad the
sea's gone, surely? It's beautiful . . .
it's . . . it's . . . bigger than any of us!"
 "Give them time," whispered the
Sea. "Wait till the weather starts to
change. Wait till the rain stops falling
and the rivers and lakes start to dry
up. Wait till it starts to get really hot.
Then they'll see what good their roads
and office blocks and supermarkets

will do them."

"No," said Henry, frightened now. "You wouldn't let that happen." He stared at the dingy grey bottle in his lap. "Would you, Sea?"

"It depends," said the Sea, a little haughtily, but glad all the same that Henry cared so much. "Depends on how I'm feeling."

"Shush," said Henry's mum, thinking it was Henry who was speaking. "Listen to this!" The news was still droning on on the radio:

'*Meanwhile,*' the newsreader gargled – this time it sounded as if he had pebbles in his mouth, not prunes – '*the police hunt for the sea continues. Detectives are being helped in their enquiries by a number of anxious fish, but admit that the*

scale of this investigation may yet
defeat them. The police are particularly
eager to talk to the owner of a pale
blue family saloon currently heading
for the coast, accompanied by what one
commentator described as, "not so
much a flock of seagulls as a swarm." '

49

"Eh?" Henry's dad turned round to glance at Henry on the back seat. "That's us. There can't be two cars on the motorway with the sort of bird problem we've got."

"Watch where you're going," Henry's mum urged as the sound of three or four blaring car horns penetrated the fog of seagulls. "Let's try to get home safely."

"Even when I watch, I can't see anything," Henry's dad grunted in reply. "I'd stop the car, but I don't know where the side of the road is."

What Happened While The Sea Was Gone

AFTER A TIME, the cloud of seagulls
thinned slightly and from the back of
the car, Henry saw where they were.

"We're almost home," he said.
"Look, there's the pier and the helter-
skelter."

"And there's the beach," said
Henry's dad. "Lots of beach – that's
all there is."

"Except you can hardly see it," said
Henry's mum. "Look!"

And Henry looked.

"Oh no!" he yelled. "What have
they done?"

Through the car window – and through a whole crowd of onlookers and TV cameras and police and builders with hard hats and walkie-talkies – Henry glimpsed barricades and hoardings where once the waves had broken. Large signs announced things like: 'COMING SOON – A NEW RESIDENTIAL COMPLEX' and 'SITE ACQUIRED FOR MONEYSPINNER, YOUR FRIENDLY NEIGHBOURHOOD SUPERSTORE – PARKING NO PROBLEM.' Through gaps in the hoardings, he could see cranes and earth-diggers ready to go to work on the endless miles of pebbles and sand and rocks which stretched to the horizon.

"Can you see any of this, Sea?" he whispered.

"I can," said the Sea.

"I can't believe it," Henry said.

"I can," said the Sea.

"There's our house," Henry's father announced. "I've never been so glad to be home. It's going to take me a week to scrape the car clean."

"There seem to be two police cars waiting for us, dear," Henry's mother remarked. "I think that grim-faced

gentleman on the doorstep with the anorak and dark glasses must be some sort of detective, don't you?"

"But I've paid my parking tickets," grumbled Henry's dad. "All except the last. What can they want?"

"I think I know," Henry said a little shakily, as he struggled to push the bottle containing the Sea under his father's car seat. "Stay out of sight, Sea," he whispered. "I think we may have trouble."

A Nose For Trouble

THE DETECTIVE WAS just like all the
street-smart cops Henry had seen on
television. In fact, although the
detective would never have admitted
it, he was just like all the street-smart
cops he himself had seen on television!
He talked to Henry's mum and dad,
but something – some instinct for
getting to the root of a problem – kept
bringing him back to Henry.

"I've got a nose for trouble, sonny,"
he told Henry, tapping it with two
fingers and pushing his dark glasses
up on to his forehead. "I'm like a

bloodhound," he went on. "I can sniff out the truth. And something here smells fishy to me."

"Oh, that smell has been in the air ever since the sea vanished," Henry said. "It's probably what's been attracting the seagulls."

The detective looked rather doubtfully at Henry. "Yes, the seagulls," he said. "It was them what

drew us to you. Can you explain why, of all the cars on the road in the past two days, the seagulls chose your dad's vehicle to follow? I've heard of seagulls following a ship before, but never a family saloon. It's a bit of a mystery, innit?"

"Yes," Henry agreed. "It is."

"You wouldn't know anything about what's been going on, I suppose?" The detective chewed his lip a bit, the way he had seen one of his heroes on TV do, and let his dark glasses slip back down on to his nose.

"No," Henry said. He could see a policeman outside in the street talking to his dad, as his dad attacked the mess on the car with a wet sponge and a plastic scraper. Henry hoped the policeman wouldn't want to look inside the car — and particularly not

under the front seat!

Inside Henry's living room, the detective was wishing his dark glasses weren't quite so dark as they made it difficult to watch Henry closely, and he had a feeling about this strange young lad.

"Listen, sonny," he said and he took the glasses right off and bent down so as to look Henry in the eye. "I'm going to take you into my confidence, right? It's not every day a whole ocean disappears and this case could be a big break for me. I've a hunch you know more than you're telling, so I'm going to level with you. If you have any idea where the sea might be, you'd best tell me, because there are some pretty powerful people out there who want to know! This isn't just a missing cat we're talking about here. The powers that be have decided they don't want the ocean back – not like it was before, anyway. The land's too valuable, see. So when we find it – and find it we will – we're supposed to hand it over to these Royal Navy scientist chappies.

"I gather the Navy rather feels it was caught with its trousers down when this all happened. As I understand it, the plan is to miniaturise the sea and keep our bit of it in a large paddling pool somewhere to the left of North Wales, where the

Navy can play with their boats in peace."

The detective straightened up and shook his head in wonderment at the people who managed affairs of this scale. "So you see, laddy, we're talking big bananas here and it's not going to do you any good or me any good if you hold out on me now . . . " He peered at Henry expectantly.

"But I don't know anything," Henry said. He could feel sweat running down his forehead and hoped the detective wouldn't notice. He wished the man would go away – he made Henry distinctly nervous – but then he noticed that the detective was sweating too and realised just how hot the day had become. He recalled what the Sea had said about the weather changing and wondered if this was the start of it. If so – was it already too late? Henry hoped not.

"Well, you think about what I've said." Sighing resignedly, the detective gave Henry a pat on the shoulder and turned to go. "I'm sure you're a sensible lad and if you have a change of heart, you know where to reach me."

"Oh yes," said Henry. He watched from the doorstep as the detective said goodbye to his father, who was still scraping the car clean. The uniformed policeman was already waiting in the police car and Henry wiped his brow with relief as the detective got in and they drove off. At least the Sea was still safe!

Friends

THAT NIGHT, WHILE Henry's mum and dad sat watching TV, Henry crept out to the car and smuggled his friend inside the house and up to his room.

"Sea," he said. "Are you all right?"

"I'm all right," said the Sea, "but I think this cardboard bottle or whatever it is is getting rather soggy. Do you think – ?"

"Of course," said Henry. And he poured the Sea out of the papier-mâché urine bottle and into his best blue *Aardvaark Attack – Return Of The*

Sand Cadets beach bucket, which he had got free with a Megaburger and a chocolate-chip milkshake.

Staring at the Sea in the bottom of the bucket, Henry thought it looked somehow diminished in size. "Are you still all there, Sea?" he asked. "I mean, there's not less of you or anything, is there? You're not shrinking?"

"Don't worry," said the Sea. "I may have evaporated a little, but there's still enough of me left to perform the other half of my party trick – if I decide to go back!"

"If?!" Henry repeated. "If?! You've got to. You heard what they're planning to do . . . build things everywhere and make roads and golf courses and supermarkets! And – and – and there's a plan to keep you small! The Navy wants to lock you up in a paddling pool and sail boats on you and there won't be any whales left. You've got to go back. There are so many people counting on you."

"Oh, people," said the Sea.

And as if on cue, they heard the voice of another newsreader coming from the television downstairs, muffled by the floorboards of Henry's bedroom:

'In a dramatic turn of events late tonight,' the newsreader was

saying, 'the United Nations revealed that there had been a punch-up in the general assembly today over who owned which bits of the landmass uncovered by the missing sea. The American representative came to blows with our own British delegate over precisely where the newly extended State of New York stopped and the county of Cornwall began. Tiny Amsterdam Island, meanwhile, formerly located in the middle of the Indian Ocean, was today arguing that its new borders stretch from South Africa in the west

to Australia in the east and up as far
north as Sri Lanka. A United Nations
spokesperson admitted that the spectacle
of grown delegates throwing
sandwiches at one another and pouring
salt in each other's coffee was highly
deplorable, not to mention downright
embarrassing.'

"You see?" Henry said. "We need
you. You've got to go back, otherwise
there'll be chaos."

"But I like it here," the Sea said,
glancing round Henry's room and
admiring the cut of Henry's
varnished-oak bunk beds, which
reminded him of sailing ships of old.
"I've never had a friend like you. I
don't want to lose you."

"You won't lose me," Henry said,
and although he tried to stop them, he

felt tears sneak into the corners of his eyes, salty-wet like the Sea. "But you've got the whole world to think of."

"The world's not such an impressive place, you know," the Sea replied. "I can stretch out and touch every part of it if I care to, but one place doesn't differ so much from the next. I can talk to you, that's what's important. You understand."

And neither of them said anything for a while. They sat in the dark in Henry's room, listening to the murmur of Henry's parents' TV from downstairs and the occasional night-time cry of a seagull drifting in on the warm breeze from outside.

Then finally the Sea said: "I haven't had a chance to ask you, you've been taking such good care of

me. Are you all right? Did the
hospital tell you how your tests
were?"

"Oh, the tests went well," Henry
said, sounding happier. "I don't have
to go back for six months – and if I'm
fine then, there won't be any more
tests for a year. No more hospital!" he
added, and smiled.

He hesitated, then reached for the
blue bucket. He took hold of the
handle. "Come on, Sea," he said.
"We've got to go."

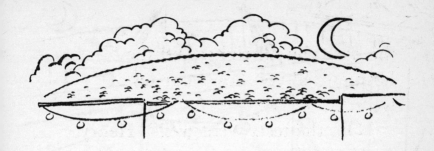

The Beach After Dark

THE BEACH LOOKED quite different in the dark. Not that it was entirely dark; the moon was out and there were electric lights at strategic points along the builders' hoardings.

"What does that sign say?" the Sea asked. "I can't make it out."

Henry read slowly: " 'WARNING – GUARD DOGS ON PATROL.' "

"You'd better be careful," said the Sea. "I don't want you getting hurt."

Henry carried his bucket with the Sea in it along the endless fence the barricades and hoardings created.

"This is terrible," he said. "I can't even get close to where you used to be."

"You could try throwing me over the top of those hoardings," the Sea suggested. "Only, you probably couldn't throw high enough. Why don't you just tip me out on to the ground here and I'll trickle under? I'll find a way."

"No," said Henry. "I want to do this properly."

"Well, don't take too long," the Sea told him. "You shouldn't be out this late on your own. Your parents would be worried sick if they knew."

Henry smiled in the moonlight. "I'm all right," he said. "I'm with you."

Someone Is Taking The Video Games Away

THERE WAS A light at the entrance to
the pier. Henry could just make out
the huge metal legs reaching out over
where the Sea used to be, casting
frightening shadows onto the beach
below.

As he got closer with his bucket, he
saw that an iron grille now closed off
most of the access to the pier and a
security guard stood where it was still
open, talking to a man in dark
overalls.

"That's most of them loaded up
now," the man in overalls was saying.

"We've got all the video games on the truck. The dodgems went this morning. That leaves the helter-skelter, the kiddies' motorbikes and the ghost train."

Henry hid himself behind a closed hamburger stand, well out of sight of the two men.

"What'll happen to you then, mate?" the man in overalls asked the guard. "You losing your job, too?"

"Nah," the guard replied. "No problem. There may not be much call for a pier without water, but they'll always need reliable security personnel like myself. The company that owns this pier is going to redevelop it into a clubhouse for the new golf course. I'm staying on."

"That would make your dad happy," the Sea whispered to Henry. "A new golf course!"

"Shhh," Henry said.

"What was that?" the man in overalls asked. "I must be working too late. Sounded like . . . like . . . a wave breaking or something."

"The strain's getting to you," joked the guard. "Probably just one of them seagulls overhead. Look at them all – I didn't know they flew at night." He leaned his head back and shouted up

at the birds, laughing: "HAVEN'T
YOU GOT A HOME TO GO TO?"

Henry, meanwhile, had picked up
an old drinks can from under his feet.
Setting the Sea down for a moment,
he tossed it with all his might in the
direction of the truck containing the
video games. The can hit the street
and rattled and rolled across the road.

"That was no seagull!" the man in
overalls said.

Searching around in the shadows
for something else to throw, Henry
spotted a large stone which had been
used to weigh down a tarpaulin.
When he picked it up, it was heavier

77

than he'd expected, but he managed
to swing himself round and sent it
flying off after the can. It landed with
a loud crash behind the truck.

"Who's there?" the security guard
shouted.

"Keep your hands off my
machines!" the man in overalls called
out.

"I'd better take a look," the guard
told him.

And the two of them went over to
investigate, which was exactly what
Henry had hoped they would do.
While the security guard was flashing
his torch under the truck and telling
whoever was there they'd best not
start any trouble, Henry picked up the
blue bucket containing his friend and
slipped through the entrance and on
to the pier.

The Sea Goes Whoosh Again

"I DON'T LIKE goodbyes," said the Sea as Henry walked over the dark wooden boards along the pier, past where the shooting gallery used to be and the remote-controlled motorboats. "Why don't I just stay?"

"We've been through this," Henry whispered, shivering a little as he marched bravely under the big plaster spider outside the ghost train. "I don't want you to go any more than you do, but you must. You can't let them spoil everything."

"I know." The Sea seemed to

sparkle in a sad way in the moonlight as Henry swung the bucket and walked on, past the Circus.

"You just want your video games back," the Sea teased.

"Oh, them," Henry said, glancing through the windows at the dark, empty spaces where his dragon game and the dune-buggy game and the starfighter game and all the others had stood. "I don't care about them any more," he said. "Not really."

And they were at the end of the pier, the very end, past the helter-skelter, where there was nothing to see by the moon's light, except a desert of sand and rocks and pebbles disappearing into the night.

"Home!" the Sea said, and Henry thought it sounded better than it had for some time.

"I'm going to miss you," Henry said.

"I'll be here," the Sea told him. "You can come and see me every day, like you always did."

"Yes," said Henry.

"And even when you're not here, you can think of me," the Sea went on. "Promise me this, that every night when you lie in that splendid wooden bunk of yours, you'll imagine you are

on a boat sailing around the world under the stars. No need to worry about where you're going," the Sea said. "I'll guide you."

"All right," said Henry.

He heard voices coming along the pier, which he realised must be the man in overalls and the security guard.

"Now what?" he whispered to the Sea. "Over the railing or through the boards?"

"Boards, please," the Sea said. "I've always enjoyed soaking them whenever I could."

"You're sure you can do this?" Henry asked, suddenly doubtful. "I mean, what happens if you don't know the rest of your party trick?"

"We'll just have to see, won't we?" his friend told him.

And Henry tipped the bucket –
slowly at first, then more quickly
when he heard the voices getting
closer – and emptied the Sea down
through the cracks between the
wooden boards of the pier.

"Blimey, it's a kid!" the man in
overalls said when he saw Henry.
"What are you doing here at this time
of night? Where's your mum and
dad?"

"We're shut, you know," the
security guard said, thinking this very
funny. "Even if we was open, we'd be
shut. No more seaside. No more pier."

"But look!" Henry said.

As he spoke, there was that sound
again – a great rush of water all
moving at once, exciting and
frightening at the same time.

"Listen!" Henry said.

And when the great whoosh died down, there was a new sound in the air, a lapping and a rolling . . . the sound of waves washing onto the beach.

"Blimey!" said the man in overalls again. "It's back. The sea – it's back!"

And Henry stood with the two men and stared out from the end of the pier at the sea in the moonlight.

"There's nothing quite like it, is there?" the man in overalls muttered as they watched white breakers ride in, like ghost horses galloping on the water.

After a while, the security guard turned to Henry and said, "Well, we'd better get you home."

"I'd like that," Henry told him.

He picked up his bucket and

walked with them both the length of
the pier. As he looked down through
the cracks in the boards and glimpsed
the Sea foaming on the pebbles below,
Henry whispered, "Goodbye, Sea. I'll
come and see you again tomorrow."

And the Sea didn't say anything. It
just waved goodbye.